Pluto

Gulzar

Poet, author, lyricist, film-maker, screenplay and dialogue writer, Gulzar is one of the towering figures of Indian cinema, culture and literature. Born in Dina (now in Pakistan), his career in cinema took off as an assistant to legendary film-maker Bimal Roy with whom he debuted as a lyricist in *Bandini* (1963). Gulzar's first film as a director was *Mere Apne* (1971). Over the next decade and a half, he made some of the most loved films of Hindi cinema, including *Aandhi*, *Parichay*, *Mausam*, *Ijaazat* and *Maachis*, among others. Apart from being a film-maker with a difference, he was undoubtedly the finest lyricist of his time, penning some of the most enduring songs of Hindi cinema.

A stalwart of Indian literature and one of the finest poets in Urdu/ Hindustani, his poetry collections include *Pukhraj*, *Raat Pashmine Ki*, *Triveni*, *Yaar Julahe*, *Pandrah Paanch Pachattar*, and a number of works translated into English: *Selected Poems*, *Neglected Poems* and *Green Poems*. As a short story writer he has a number of volumes to his credit, including *Ravi Paar* and *Dhuaan*. He is also one of the finest writers for children in the country.

He has won the Filmfare Award twenty times, the National Award seven times and has been a recipient of the Sahitya Akademi Award and the Padma Bhushan. In 2008, he was awarded an Oscar for his song '*Jai ho*' in *Slumdog Millionaire* and also received a Grammy for the same in 2010. He received the Dadasaheb Phalke Award in 2014.

Nirupama Dutt

Nirupama Dutt is a poet, journalist, literary and art critic and translator of many seasons who has written and edited several books. She writes in both Punjabi and English. She received the Punjabi Akademi Award for her anthology of poems, *Ik Nadi Sanwali Jahi*. At present she is translating three novellas by Amrita Pritam and working on a novel of her own.

PLUTO

Gulzar

Translated by
Nirupama Dutt

HarperCollins *Publishers* India

First published in India in 2015 by
HarperCollins *Publishers* India

HarperCollins Publishers India, Cyber City, Building 10-A, Gurugram,
Haryana-122002, India
www.harpercollins.co.in

1 2 3 4 5 6 7 8 9 10

P-ISBN: 978-93-5136-508-2
E-ISBN: 978-93-5136-509-9

Typeset in 12/15 Requiem Text Regular at
SURYA, New Delhi

Printed and bound in India at MicroPrints Inida, New Delhi

Printed and bound at
MicroPrints India, New Delhi

MIX
Paper
FSC FSC® C218906

This product is made of FSC®-certified and other controlled material.

HarperCollins Publishers, Macken House, 39/40 Mayor Street
Upper, Dublin 1, D01 C9W8, Ireland

Vishal! Vishal Bhardwaj...
Where do we go next?

Contents

A Note on Pluto by Gulzar *xi*
Translator's Note *xiii*

For a Long Time 3
Had I Not Left Her... 4
Mid-sky 5
A While Longer 6
I Looked at You 7
Sometimes 8
Tell Him 9
Branded 10
Lost and Found I 11
Lost and Found II 12
I Have Complained, But... 13
Why Are Your Hands... 14
And You Were Gone 15
When You Went Away 16
She Was Alive 17
Meena 18
Enveloped in Mist, Again 19
Feasting in the Sky 20
Moon Slate 21
Cloud Catchers 22
Weaving a Night 23
Not a Good Habit 24
Butterflies 25
Gate 26
Unseasonal 27

Pali 28
The Evening Is an Interlude 31
The Trees Every Evening 32
Cigarette 33
Why 34
Under My Door 35
Boarding Card 36
Sometimes... 37
Horizon 38
Dirty Ragged Dawn 39
Forlorn, Widowed Voices 40
Ever So Slowly 41
A Year 42
On the Moon 45
A Search 46
Kudremukh Lake 47
Betrayal 48
Prayer Beads 49
A Tiny Globe 50
A Book of a Bygone Era 51
Whirlwind 52
Changing Course 53
Tunnel 54
Reflection 57
A Thought 58
Balm 59
Analysing a Poem 60
My Drinking Buddy 61
Amrita–Imroz 62
A Season for Poems 63

A Thought, Buried 64
My Friend, the Poet 65
Blank Page 66
Breakfast 67
Faith 71
Still Life 72
Bandra 73
Goa 74
Chamba 75
A Matter of Habit 76
Birds or Flags 77
Crossings 78
Runway 81
Birds on the Runway 82
Belgian Crystal Ware 83
By Air 84
A Walk in the Clouds 85
No Smoking 89
Baba, My Messiah 90
A Feverish Image 91
Hope 92
Ties That Bind 93
Curtains 94
Please Tell Allama... 95
Returning Home 96
Pedicure 97
Holding My Hand 98
Scene 1 99
Scene 2 100
Dreams 101

Sunlight 102
Cracked Cup 103
Graveyard 104
Scene 3 105
Holding Up the Sky 106
Coming Apart 107
A Tale of Two Roads 108
The Forsaken Cage 109
The Chase 110
The Well of Silence 111
Silences 112
Footpath 113
Joseph's Right Shoulder 114
Tattoo 115
Nowhere to Go 116
Shadow 117
Man-eater 118
Rusted Moon 119
Hustle-Bustle 120
Tapi 121
Tradition 122
Fame 123
Abuse 124
Lamplight 125
Morning Walk 126
Garland 127

A Note on Pluto

Gulzar

Pluto lost its status as a planet recently. Scientists said: 'Away with you. We will not include you in our family of nine planets ... you are not one!'

I had lost my place long ago when my family said, 'How come a *mirasi* in a family of businessmen?'

Silence echoed that you are not one of us.

My heart is saddened at Pluto's sorrow on being rejected thus. It is so far away ... so tiny ... so all my 'pint-sized' poems I gift to it.

Some moments are fleeting, ephemeral. We often fail to grasp them. I like to hoard them. As far as the themes are concerned, many poems in this collection are unconventional ... but then that is not such a bad thing, is it?

Translator's Note

Gulzar sahib is an artist of the little things that matter: the short fleeting moments that he captures so originally and the small wonders that still excite him. This comes through most spontaneously in the short poems that the poet dedicated to Pluto, the planet that was banished from its family of planets! It is the metaphor of exile that he celebrates in many ways in this collection which looks at the grim and the joyous, the ordinary and the extraordinary, the stagnant and the fluid, the amusing and the annoying with the poetic flourish so typical of him. It was sheer pleasure to be on this journey through seas, mountains, ponds, trees, clouds, the bedroom window, the deep recesses of the heart and the agility of a sharp mind finding expressions to match his spontaneous and masterly brief tryst with words. And these words are not mere words but a flight of ideas. My salaam to Gulzar sahib and to the poetic impulse that makes the long journey of life worth the trouble.

Nirupama Dutt

Verification

Ask about the chassis
Its date of manufacture
Else, the salesman will cheat.

The date on mine reads:
18 August 1934!

Such a long journey through silences
So many things have I tried to tell her...

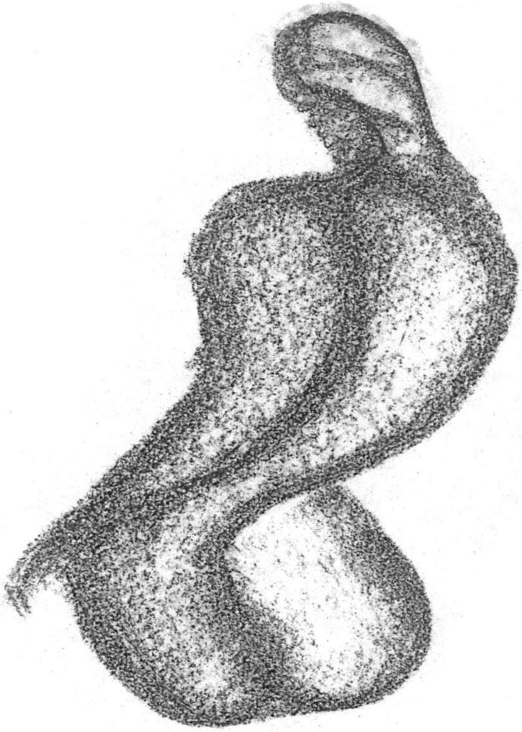

For a Long Time

For an eternity your sorrow buried in my heart
Has been biting me on my tongue.
Draping the snake around my neck like Shiva
I have drifted for ages,
Denied rest, refused sleep.

Your sorrow now finds repose
In the sanctuary of a poem.

Had I Not Left Her...

Had I not left her, she would have.

Intimacy and separation are elemental in love
But what do you do with ego that pricks every time you turn?
After all, one cannot lie on one's back all night.

Mid-sky

And as we talked,
The moon, mid-sky,
Went out suddenly,
Like a candle flame
Blown away...

Listen love,
Do not sigh so deep!

A While Longer

If only you had stayed a while longer...
To catch the drop of sun
That slipped from your earring
To kiss your face...

But you turned away
And it fell and shattered on the floor.

If only you had stayed a while longer...

I Looked at You

I looked at you like everyone else did
But then it so transpired
On my way back
The memory of your face lit up my eyes.

Shaken by a gust of breeze, a flame fell.
Momentary darkness – and then
A blaze which turned into a forest fire.

Sometimes

Sometimes
You fall silent while saying something.
A freeze frame
In the din of a film.
The hush takes you suddenly
It falls upon your eyes.

I touch your silence
To read its fragile Braille of things unsaid.

Tell Him

'Tell him...'
She whispered, head bowed,
Her toe scraping the earth
As if searching for
The core of what she wanted to say...

She kept silent,
Stifled a sob
Then lifted her head and looked away
And said once more:
'Just tell him this...'

Branded

Kissing your face
Against the glass
Oh! How have I been branded!
As if your face has been imprinted on mine!

I wander this city wearing your face
And people ask me about your well-being.

Lost and Found I

Suddenly, I saw you
On this flight today. So alone.
And then saw you approach
The 'Lost and Found'.

Ah!
You still haven't lost
Your habit of losing anything.

Lost and Found II

I came to the 'Lost and Found'
To a list of things misplaced in the flight.
The official laughed when I said,
'What if I gave you just a name? Or a photograph?'

But he laughed on
And missed the tears welling up in my eyes.

I Have Complained, But...

I have complained, but...
Only to feel it ebb.

If only I had kept it to myself
Let it fester,
Raw and untreated,
It would have grown to a wound!

But, dejected, I complained.
And ebbed further away.

Why Are Your Hands...

Why are your hands so silent?
Neither do they reach out to me
When you sit at the edge of the bed,
Nor do they call out softly
From across the windowpane.
They don't rise to rebuke me, either.

Forever still
I see them always, like a flame lit,
Invoking God.

What have the doctors told you?

And You Were Gone*

It was all too sudden
When you went away.
A power cut. Instant darkness.
And I, in this closed room,
Getting used to it,
See the edges of the door outlined.

---

*With apologies to Dr Bashir Badr

When You Went Away

Bereft of you, the eyes are but lenses devoid of light.
With what do I comfort them?
When awake, they stare at blank pages.
Otherwise, they drape themselves in a restless sleep
And spend the night licking arid dreams.

Whatever will happen to these orphaned eyes?
Without you, they are but useless, benighted glasses.

She Was Alive

She lived when I was asleep
Died, when I woke up.
Such is the nature of dreams.

How many times, then, will she return?
How many times will I let her die?

Meena

She closed her eyes:
And died
And never breathed again.
After a life as long,
Eventful and intricate,
The end, so silent and simple.

Enveloped in Mist, Again

Once more, the mist claims it
Once more, the shadows grow thick
Once more, it melts away
Drop by drop, the face fades...
Memories ripple a while before drowning.
My eyes are moist once again.

Feasting in the Sky

The banquet above us is aglitter
With its gleaming silver dish
The twinkle of platinum rice
Against the spread, deep azure.

This feast would be perfect
Only if you join me.
I would offer you the chalice of moonlight.

Moon Slate

When my fingers tire
Of chalking on the moon
I write the rest of the letter
With the light of my eye.

I believe that on full-moon nights
She comes to the terrace,
Draped in a 'garad' sari,
To worship the moon.

Cloud Catchers

Hold one end of the cloud
While I spread the other
And tying it to the ends of a rainbow
Swing under its seven-hued arch.

Let's ask the sun to rock the swing
Up and across the sky.
Will you join me?

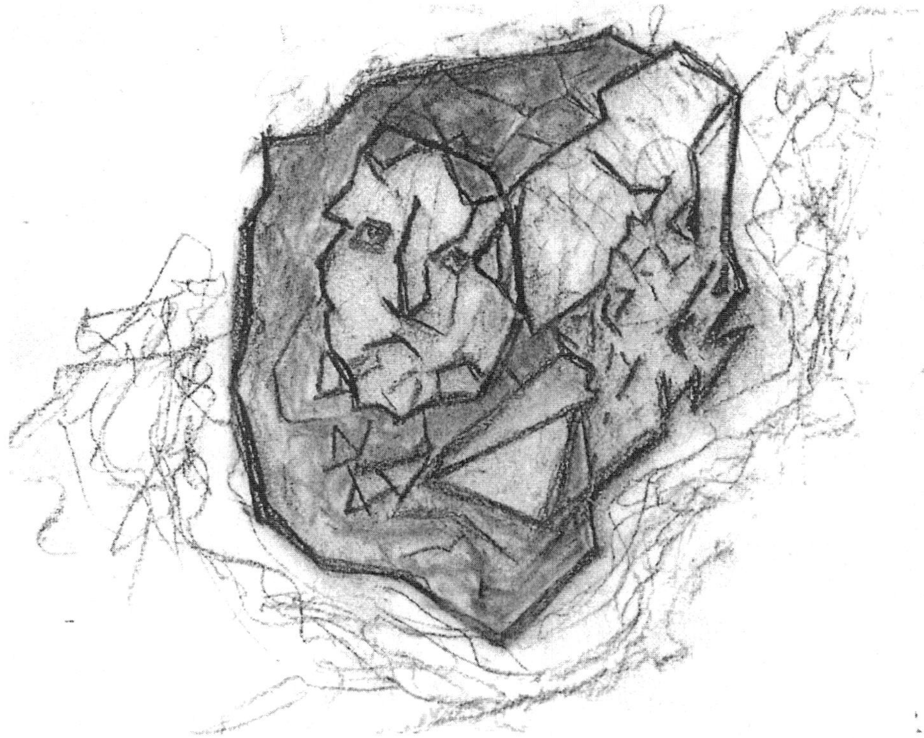

Weaving a Night

The blanket of night
I wove for the world
Fell short...

Now it slips away from one end or the other.

You draw it over you when you tire
And leave me awake in solitude.

Not a Good Habit

Spring leaves the sky blushing
A twinge of twilight rose.
And in its bloom
It ripens with passion.

This is what youth is all about.
When it arrives
One cannot help teasing the sky.

Butterflies

Butterflies flit across
Leaping high and low,
From the 'arohi' to 'avrohi',
Scaling the seven notes of music.

Slumbering clouds toss and rumble,
As palm trees wave and sway.

It is birthday time in Aurangabad
With Boski and Govind!

Gate

The sandalwood tree
Stands guard at the gate.
Every time I enter
A branch bends over my eye.
I have pushed it away often
Only to have it whisper in my ear.

Sandalwood is so very fragrant
But bereft of flowers.

Unseasonal

Only the other day my younger son
Brought an anaar, leftover
From a Diwali of yesteryears.

Its spark and dazzle,
Out of season, devoid of context,
Accentuated the silence in the courtyard.

Your letter arrived, seasons old.

Pali*

Death stalks
Waiting in the shadows to pounce.
Pali, frail and sick,
Now its inevitable prey.

Devoid of faith, bereft of religion
Death devours but everything.

---

*My Boxer dog

Perhaps, a moment has stopped midway
Perhaps time has tied itself in a knot

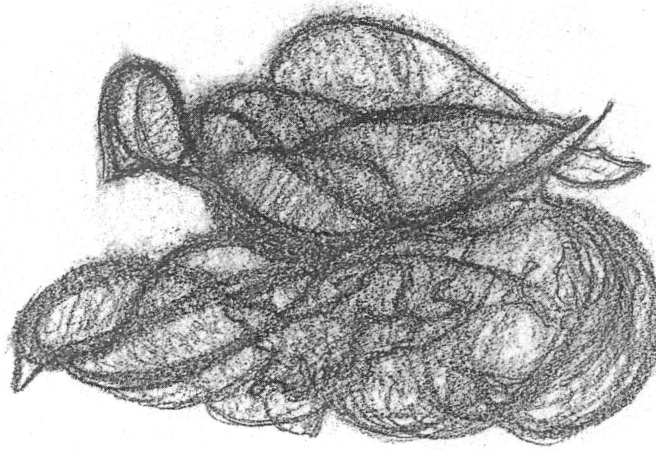

The Evening Is an Interlude

The evening is but a pause,
A cold sigh
Or a new paragraph.

All days and nights pause here
Time turns over and continues the narrative.
The evening is but a pause.

The Trees Every Evening

The trees cradle the shavings of day
Only to wave and cast it away
Over the green shoulders of the hills.

But the day grows back again
In the solitude of night,
Sprouting from the branches
I had sawed and felled.

Cigarette

The cigarette,
Glowing between my fingers,
The sun's farewell just a puff or two away.

The sea asked of me one last drag
And in the pause between the puff
I saw the day grow ashen.

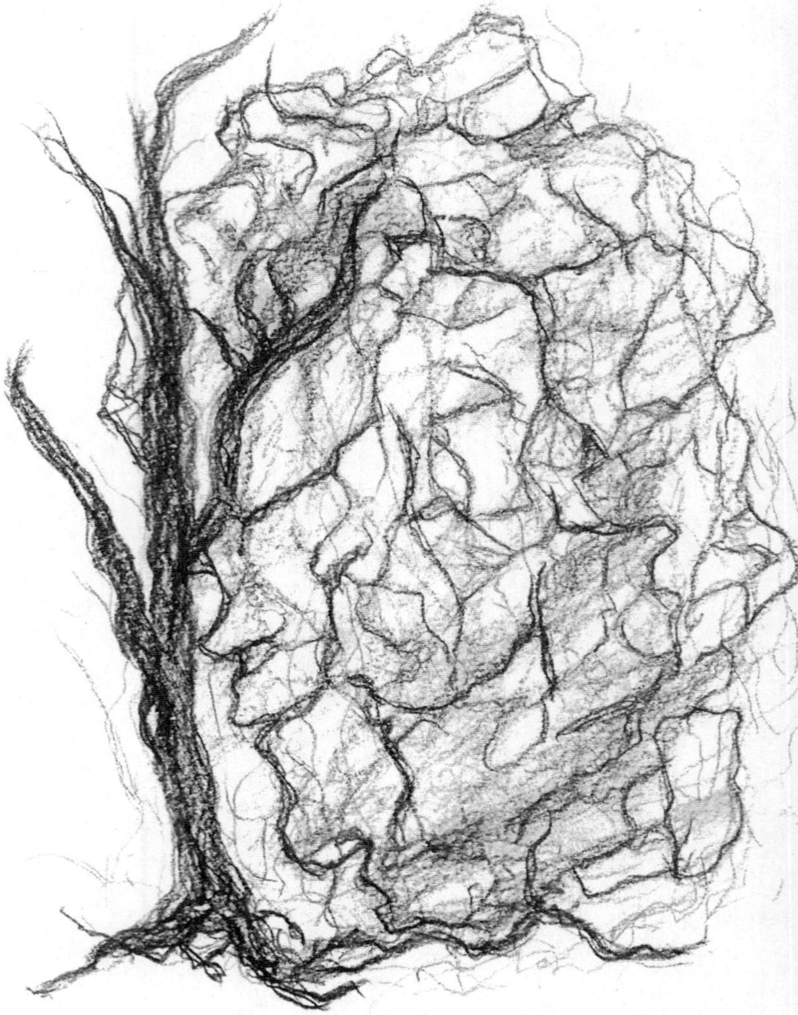

Why

Why live in a city
Where the day is butchered.
Skinned alive, and its flesh put on sale?
The poor day whines
And drags itself to the slaughter house
Before the final hour.

Under My Door

Is there a fissure under my door?
Through which darkness seeps into my room
Like after an ink-spill
Or does night hover over the courtyard, its taps open?
The room floods over.

Boarding Card

This cut-out of the moon
Staring from an ancient, serrated sky
Resembles a boarding card
Blowing across the runway.
Abandoned perhaps
By someone who missed his flight
Or simply, changed his mind.

Sometimes...

Sometimes, the moon peeks
From behind the mountains
And measures the snow.

If all is clear, it will summon the flock
One by one, they come out, shy little stars
Some wrapped in a woolly haze,
Others a-shiver, sneaking away from the moonlight.

The herd glitters all over the sky
Until their shepherd comes calling, 'Hoosh, hoosh...'
And herds them home.

Horizon

You can see it in the horizon
The ink-black cat emerging.
Its face caressing the twilight
Which will soon turn red-hot, sipping the sun.

It licks its whiskers
Slick with yellow tongue
Lifts a corner of the night
And escapes towards tomorrow's dawn.

Dirty Ragged Dawn

Dawn breaks, grimy and bruised
The sky looms tattered

As though a cat had trampled
That sheet of sky
With paws, wet and dirty.

Forlorn, Widowed Voices

Often, forlorn, widowed voices
Echo from the mosque's backyard
Linger on the brick wall
Wail with parched lips against stone-deaf ears
A requiem for a primal Allah
Who placed the human race in their wombs
And retired to a silence known to the grave.

Ever So Slowly

Slowly, ever so slowly, the bottle has emptied out.
We drank of this year, sip by sip
Each swig, a taste of fire,
It left our lips scorched.

A Year

Slowly, the earth rolls back to its original home.
And Venus, Saturn, Rahu and Ketu all retreat to their own.

For a year the universe revolved around me
And on the eighteenth day of August
Reclaimed its place!

An ancient temple
A lamp flickers at dusk...

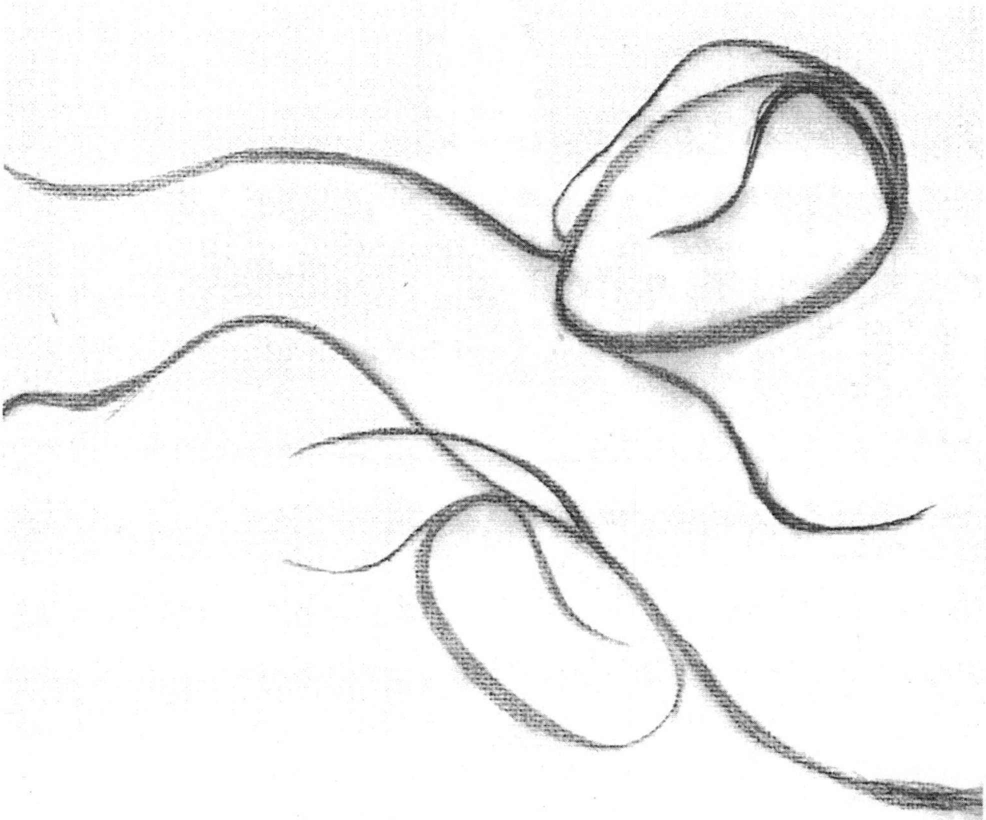

On the Moon

We arrived, not too long ago,
Here, to reside on the moon.
Neither water, nor breeze,
Not a speck of garbage anywhere, bereft of all life
And devoid of gravity, the body weightless.

Come, let's go back,
No matter its failings,
To earth, let us return.

A Search

The earth continues on its way around the sun
Tagging me along
I scan the whole universe with the searchlight
For a face, a name, an address nowhere to be found.

Kudremukh Lake

Trees stand sedate,
Serene as Buddhist monks in prayer
Knee deep in water, arms raised
To a sky too clear
Calling out for one who does not reside there.

Betrayal

How my body betrays me!

We were together the other day
Scaling the mountains
As black-masked clouds pounced upon us.

The body climbed down
The mist of a waterfall,
Leaving me stranded in space!

Prayer Beads

The earth chants over a beaded loop
Of nights and days, its rosary
Year after year it circles the sun
Three billion have passed.
The Lord slumbers still.

When the fire within cools
And is about to go out
He will open eyes of crimson fire
And welcome the mendicant life
To the warmth of his embrace.

A Tiny Globe

Anywhere I seek to keep my stuff
In this tiny globe available to me
I find someone else staking a claim.

I'm afraid to unpack my belongings.
What if I find Him there too?
Wish there was a corner devoid of Him!

He has encroached upon
Every bit of space available on this earth!

A Book of a Bygone Era

God is a book of eras past
Wrapped in a sacred cloth
Left to wait on a pedestal
For only the chosen to read.

Today, it has become so mundane
One finds it lying around
Like an old magazine
In the waiting room of a clinic.

Whirlwind

The earth spins, a whirlwind,
Stop it!
Let me get off
And find my rightful place.

Every year it brings me to
That same old station: my birthdate
And it does not stop.

If Time spreads
Where does one find the shore?
If the space shrinks
Where is the core?

Changing Course

Surely we could leave this path
For a new one, unlike it.

They say, He has our route mapped out
Just like a contractor hiring workers at a building site
And calling them back at end of day.

Surely, there must be other maps
To choose from the universe.
A different master of our destines,
Surely, another god.

Tunnel

If only for a moment, close your eyes.
As you cross the tunnel
Your body will be left behind.
Bedazzled by the blinding light beyond
You'll never again need to open your eyes.

If it bleeds, it is but a wound
Otherwise, every hurt is a poem

Reflection

A drop or the sea itself.
When still, it holds in itself all it sees
Mirroring everything in its glass eyes, wide.

A poet is a drop of water
Tiny spec, endless reflection.

A THOUGHT

That one thought
Sharp as a razor's edge
Sears through flesh
And tiny tributaries of blood boil over.

Once cool, like spring water
They quench this verdant verse
And let the poem bloom.

BALM

I weave these words
Knots and gauzes of a poem
And use it as a bandage to staunch
The tears of a slit vein.

They dull the edge of the sword
But cannot soak dry
The blood seeping out of the wound.

Analysing a Poem

To analyse a poem
Is to strip the metaphor-petals
Of a rose in full bloom,
Until only the word-stems remain
With little more than thorns.

A fragrance lingers on the hand
Some of it lost to the breeze
The poem now resonates
Like an empty vessel, cold.

My Drinking Buddy

My poem keeps me company
As I nurse my drink in the evening.
I take a swig or two
While my friend partakes
Of the elixir late into the night.

Yet, the poem holds its drink well
While I emerge with a hangover,
Drunk on every verse for days.

Amrita–Imroz

Drifting through your poems
I am wary of
Stepping on a still-wet landscape by Imroz.

Colours drip from the brush
What emerges is the shadow of your poem.

It is as if he paints you a poem on his canvas.
It is as if you compose a painting on paper.

A SEASON FOR POEMS

Every poem has a season
If not harvested in time, it wilts.
Words wither and hang from limp metaphors.
Colours fade, and the poem
Drifts like fallen autumn leaves.

A Thought, Buried

When I buried a thought on paper
A poem opened its eyes beneath an avalanche of words!

A timid voice, faint, reaches me:
Why bury me in so many words?
Metaphors struggle in a straitjacket
In the name of art, you stifle all passion.

Does it need so many bricks to seal a thought?

My Friend, the Poet

In jest, I once asked a close poet friend:
'So, will you write a poem
Even as you breathe your last?'
He looked at me and, with a smile, said:
'It's impossible to write one before you die, my friend.
I die a million deaths for every poem I write.'

Blank Page

How long will this virgin page
Sit and stare at me, urging me wordlessly
To share the silent story etched on its face.

Will it confess if I hold it against my ear?
Will it return the kiss if I caress it with my lips?

Breakfast

The cuckoo's song
Seasons the meal, a breakfast
Fragrant with the dewy green around.
Garnished with the pale light of sunrise.

Dawn's spread had everything one could wish for
But for the tender morsel of words.
Or one could have tasted a poem.

Of course, the world outside is barren.
It is in the city that people sprout like creepers in pots.

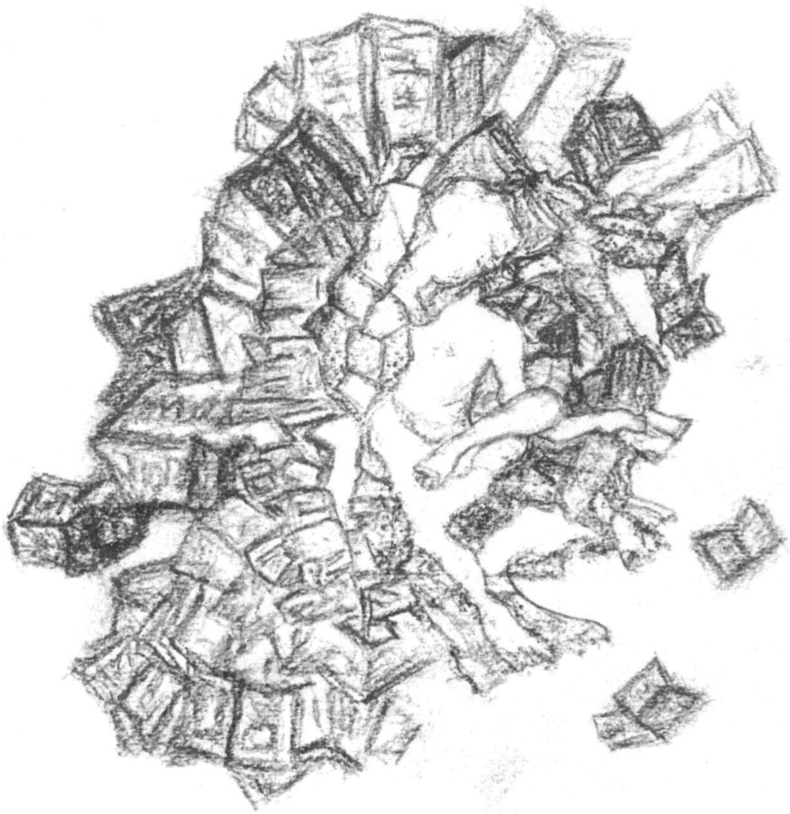

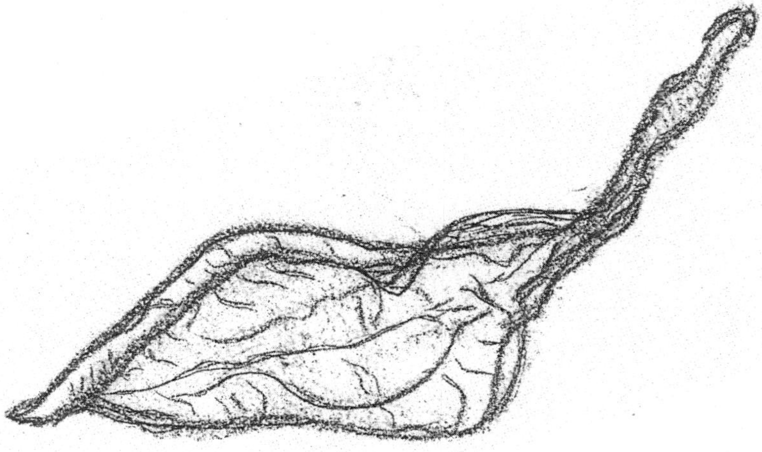

FAITH

It sat, perched on a branch
Above a pond
That held the sky in it.
Afraid of drowning,
It did not jump into the water
Neither did it fly away.
It simply withered on the branch –
That single leaf!

Still Life

It winces in apprehension on the wooden bridge
Afraid of being trampled under scurrying feet.

The dry leaf waits for the sigh of a gentle breeze
To cradle it to the river on its wings
For its one last, tranquil journey into oblivion.

Bandra

In Bandra, the sheesham tree
Stands in the pond
Stylishly braiding its branches
And like a girl curling her hair
Admires its reflection,
Swaying in the breeze.

Goa

Goa is made of warm, certain earth
Lovingly cradled by the sea.

The sea carries it on its hip
Sometimes it bobs it to the right
And then rocks it back to the left.

Like a mother, the sea swings Goa
From one hip to the other every mile or two.

Chamba

Chamba's old brown rock stands majestic
Holding in it a streak of waterfall.
Its slender course through the rock
Always reminds me of
A stray drawstring hanging loose!

A Matter of Habit

Water flows out of habit, it is fated to!

A river, always on the move.
Leaping out of crevices, a spring gushes forth.
Holding a mountain slope by its hand
A waterfall rushes down!

Tired of all the running around
Water eventually pools into deep slumber in a lake.

Birds or Flags

Are these birds? Or flags perhaps?
Could they be black badges?
The crows lining the wires
And crowding the city streets
Do they mourn the departed?
Or are they protesting an arrival?

Crossings

The train passing by
On the bridge stretched over the rivulet
Also seems to slow down, but for a moment,
Like strangers who cross each other in passing,
Pause briefly, nod at each other, before moving on.

I would have worn lightning on my sleeves
If my clothes were made of clouds.

Runway

As the airplane took off,
A crane, pecking for grains in the grass,
Cocked his neck at the smoke and sound,
Looked at the streak of fire at the tail,
And turned to its mate.
She assured him, 'It's still a baby.
It's learning to fly.'

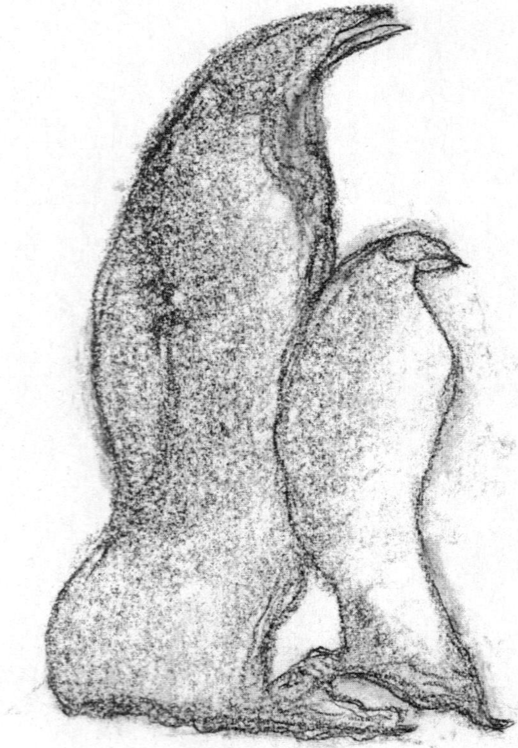

Birds on the Runway

These birds on the runway are not afraid.
It simply surprises them to see man
Try on wheels in a race to get ahead.
And fly away with the entire coop.

Daintily resting her neck on one of her wings
The wise female philosophizes to her mate:
'The poor fellows have no wings, you know.'

Belgian Crystal Ware

These clouds spread randomly
As Belgian crystal ware.
When the airplane cuts through them
Doesn't it seem that
The crystal will shatter
To a spray of shards
And its sound echo on earth?

BY AIR

In the cerulean sky
Sailing through the clouds
Nestled on a seat
Sipping hot tea,
One foot resting over the other...

No longer feels like the fantasy of Alif-Laila, does it?

A Walk in the Clouds

Come, let's open the plane's door,
Leave our socks and shoes behind
And step out, to stroll barefoot over the clouds.
Come, let's see how it feels
When feet don't touch the ground.

All of them lie shattered, in the end
Life was contained in earthen pots!

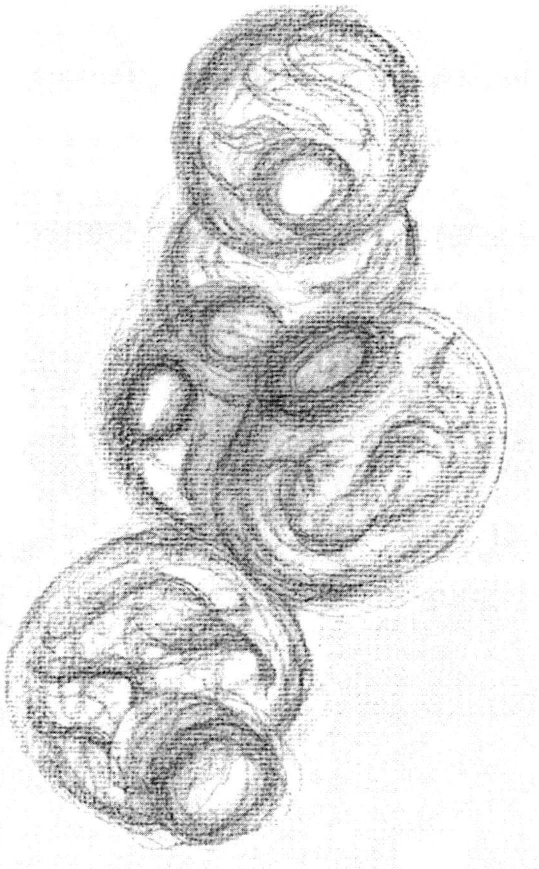

No Smoking

No, I don't smoke
But I often ask people for a light.
There's much I would like to burn
If only I could find the nerve.

Baba, My Messiah*

I see him as the Messiah
One who heals the world
Caresses its wounds away
With time and tender hope
Woven into fragile couplets
Which he serves
From the chalice of poetry.

Nothing would happen to him, I was sure
He is the Messiah.

But it did when
In Lahore, his body became his cross!

---

*Ahmed Nadeem Qasimi

A Feverish Image

Why does this image haunt me in fever:
White mattress, white pillow, my head resting on it.
White sheet, it half covers my body as I lie.
A boiled egg on a china plate.
And wafer-thin wisps of smoke!

Hope

Hope is far too slippery to grasp
It begins to melt if you hold on to it.
Rub it, and it slips through
And time rains relentlessly

Richly lathered,
This month also
Melted too soon.

Ties That Bind

The world ties me in knots
Binds me in myriad threads of love.
Throwing off the leashes that keep me grounded
How I wish I could walk barefoot in the sky.

Does the shadow of Siddhartha stalk me?

Born in Lumbini, his elongated ears
Responded to the voices from the heavens above.

Curtains

If indeed He's always watching us
Without as much as blinking
I should draw the sky-curtain
Across my window.

Why should I be answerable for His whims?

Please Tell Allama...*

Someone please tell Allama:
In the fields where the tiller goes hungry
No one burnt the crop down
No one rose, the revolution never came.

From every village now rise funeral processions
Of farmers who committed suicide
Consuming the poison of debt.

---

*In response to Allama Iqbal's lines: '*Jis khet mein dahkan to mayassar na ho roti/Uss khet ke har khosha-e-gandam to jala do*' (Burn the crop in every field/Which does not give food to its tiller)

Returning Home

Returning home from the fair
The balloon began to deflate.
The breath left its taut lung.
The face withered, wrinkled
Like grandpa's.

Pedicure

File my nails, my friends.
My feet does not need them.
They break, every time I stumble.

There are wheels on my feet.
Scrape them away too, clean off the soles.
They always drive me to wanderlust – those wheels!

Holding My Hand

Suddenly holding my hand, he said,
'We can take the narrow lane to the left.'
Before I knew what to ask of the stranger,
He called my name, pulled me into the crowd.
My hand slipped through his grasp.

The first brush with a heart attack wasn't bad!

SCENE I

The mahua blossoms are flowering once more.
And the tree is fragrant again.
In its shade, drunk on mahua
Those soldiers raped Kanchi.
From its branch, Kanchi hung herself.
The mahua blossoms are flowering once more.

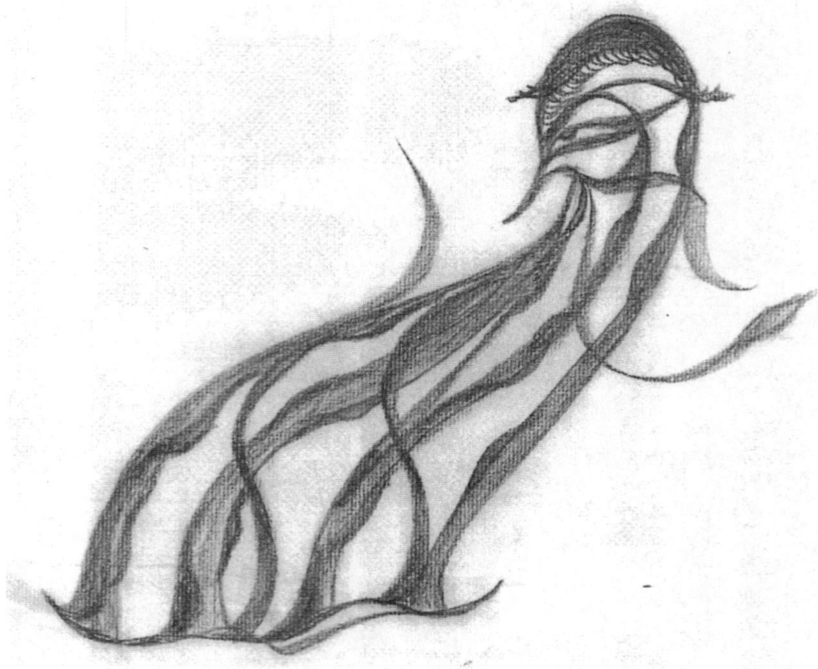

Scene 2

They call the cat Minki
From the wall she mews: 'May I?'
Kanchi's mother boils rice still
Strains it through Kanchi's veil.
Minki leaps into the courtyard and
Onto the mahua tree, surveys the scene below.
Everyone is hungry again.
The mahua blossoms are flowering once more.

Dreams

I dream, but the problem is
Their shadows do not leave my eyes
Even when I open them.

Their fragrance lingers on my lashes when I open my eyes
Before they shed their withered petals with time.
For months after, my vision is tainted ochre.

And though rivers are in spate behind my closed eyes
Once stained, dreams can never be washed clean again.

Sunlight

When sunlight's gossamer fingers
Filter through the green,
And caress the brown thigh of a tree,
I have seen the tree blush and complain:
'People misbehave and even carve
Their names on my thigh with a knife!'

I curse them ... but to no avail.

Cracked Cup

He was like a cup
With a crack running through it.
Its handle broken
And ready to singe
Lips that sip, fingers that hold.

'Away, wretched Dalit,' the boss yelled one day,
Throwing him out.

Every face in the office now bears a crack!

GRAVEYARD

A firefly hovering over
A coffin in a graveyard
Probably trying to decipher the face within.

As if one last wish of the departed soul
That somehow escaped being buried
Was trying to makes its way into the coffin.

Scene 3

The curry-stained plate
Knows these salty tears
As does the stove
Flaming with a mother-in-law's curses,
Taunts that pierce the walls.

But running her fingers
Over that wet plate
Quietly, she keeps tracing a necklace.

Holding Up the Sky

Standing at the centre of the earth
When I raised the sky with both hands,
Little did I know that
Should I ever remove them,
The sky would come crashing down.

Coming Apart

If you keep stuffing your pocket
It is bound to come apart at the seams.

One man too many, house upon house
In every town
Shops spilling onto footpaths
And by-lanes that can no longer stretch their arms.
The towns are bursting at the seams.

A Tale of Two Roads

The frail and fragile trail
Climbs every day, to the mountain summit,
While these wide concrete roads
Meander this way and that
Yet, never reach the top.

THE FORSAKEN CAGE

A cage bereft
A sliver of green pepper lies in it
And a bowl, overturned.

The bird has flown,
A prison with a story, and little more.

The Chase

Oh! The everyday race for a job
The pursuit of falling kites,
I still remember those days, Mumbai!

Rushing feet stitching the whole city together.
The crackle of dry leaves trampled under.

Running out of breath
Chasing the mirage of hope.

The Well of Silence

Step into the well of silence
Sand sodden with muffled whispers.
Pebbled words long dead
Moss clinging to the walls.

No water anywhere
Even silence is parched.

Silences

This ancient well of solitude.
The very echo of your thought
Could light up the sky.

My feet are entangled
In the quicksand of silence.

Footpath

What do the sheltered know
Of the pavement's great charms!

Blind to caste and creed, religion and faith
It breeds a hundred small truths
In alms begged of any convenient god
In festivals that speak the secular language of money.

Our god resides with us on the footpath.

Joseph's Right Shoulder

Joseph had a tattoo of
A little blue bird on his right shoulder.
He lies buried in the backyard of the Catholic church.

At dusk, a blue swallow
Comes to visit, perches by the grave.
Was the tattoo of someone the bird loved?

TATTOO

God knows why he had tattooed
A blue cow on his right shoulder.
He could have been killed in the riots!
But the rioters were considerate
Seeing the tattoo, they let him go.

Talk of bovine intervention!

Nowhere to Go*

Let's not do much today
        Just drive around the streets
Break a traffic rule or two
Block somebody's path.
Be well cursed at
Yelled at, honked at!

Anything to feel alive
Remind us that we still matter.

---

*For Vishal

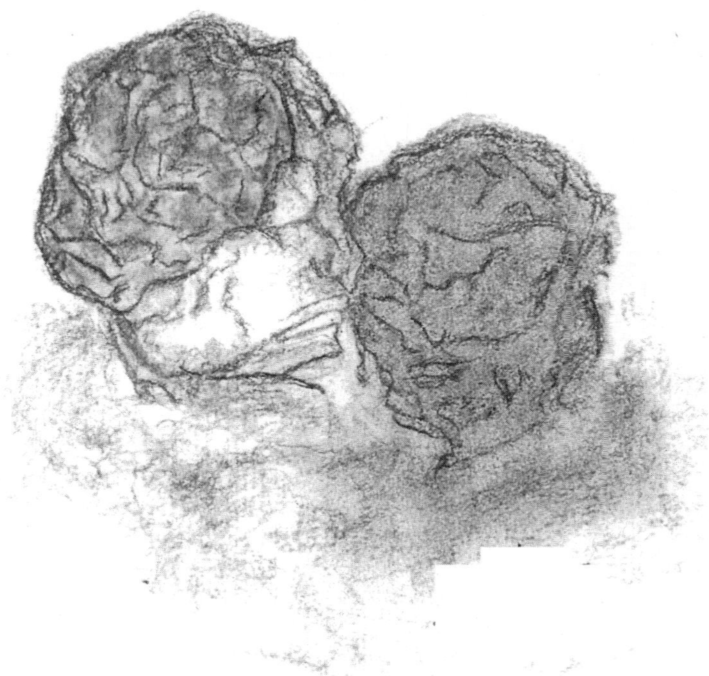

Shadow

Tramping these winding streets at night
A shadow tripped over its own shadow
Fell next to the lamppost and died.

Perhaps it too
Was the illegitimate spawn of darkness.

Man-eater

It is a man-eater
That red letterbox
In that corner out there.

Voices emerge from its cavernous belly
And yesterday, as I fed it a letter,
It gobbled up my fingers too!
That man-eater.

The red letterbox in that corner out there.

Rusted Moon

With sandpaper and a file
I have often scraped
The rust from the moon-blade
Lest it becomes blunt.

The moon-knife has to be kept sharp
To cut through the dark night.

Hustle-Bustle

Why do you lot scramble thus?
Climbing over each other.
Stop crunching my hands under your boots.
Don't ride over me,
Steamrolling my back like a road roller.

There was someone
Struggling beneath me
Till a while ago.
He now lies still!

Tapi

The banks are frothing over,
The river heaves on her back
Tapi has cholera.

She is infected with the refuse of yesterday's riots
That has flowed into her distended belly.
A night grown heavy
With the stench of scorched flesh,
She has vomited all night.
Yes, Tapi is fighting cholera.

Tradition

The glass panes lie broken
The nuts and bolts of the frame have come loose
The window struggles to break free
And fly away with the wind.

But this stone wall
          It does not give in.

Such is tradition
Hard and cold.
One might die trying
Yet fail to break free of it.

Fame

I know well how smoke stings the eye
Clouds my vision
Until I wipe the eyes clean
And am able to see once more.

You may have known of the smoke
That rises with fame
But have you seen
The fuel that has burnt within?

Abuse

His abuse
Coarse and base
Frothing in his eyes
Grating in his voice
Landing upon me
Like splattering eggs.

His words made little sense
But still my blood boiled hearing them
They hurt, but why I wonder,
As they do now and the head reels
At their very thought.

LAMPLIGHT

There is magic in lighting a lamp at dusk
The flame flutters awake, looks up
Sways in the breeze
Before it stretches, gleams
And stands brave
Daring the draught to tease it.
Yes, there is magic in lighting a lamp at dusk.

Morning Walk

They look like footballs
Those who venture out
For their morning walks.
All of them – big or small
Shrunken, bloated, stitched, ripped
And life plays with them
Dribbles, bounces
Drops, picks them up,
Kicks them from the corner post.
And those who enter the goal, never return!

GARLAND

Whom do they drape thus
With garlands that fall over my neck?

With vacant eyes they lift their hands
Eyes that conjure an image, all their own
They garland that selfsame thought.
Not me.

Whom do they drape thus
With garlands that fall over my neck?